This is My Book

Name _____

Date _____

JOHNNY TRACTOR AND FRIENDS

AFRAID OF NOTHING

CREEEEEK!

A JOHN DEERE STORYBOOK FOR LITTLE FOLKS

Kirk Barron

It was a beautiful late summer day. The afternoon sun shone down bright on Johnny Tractor and Billy Baler as they baled hay for the last time of the season.

As they rounded a curve in the field, they could
see the old Austin place. Once a grand country house,
it had long been abandoned and was rundown.

Even though they had gone right past it that morning, Johnny couldn't help but think of it every time he saw it. "You know," said Johnny, "that place is sure spooky looking." "Yeah, it gives me the willies," said Billy.

By the time they finished baling, the sun was setting and they started the trip back to farmer Tad Fowler's house. Johnny passed the old Austin house quickly. "You're not afraid, are you?" said Billy. "Who, me? I'm afraid of nothing," said Johnny proudly.

Just then a loud wailing creeeeeeeeeeeeek came from the house. The noise scared them both and Johnny ran as fast as he could almost all the way home.

"Maybe we shouldn't tell the others about that noise," said Billy. "They will think we were silly to run." "Yeah," said Johnny. "Besides, it was probably just the wind or something anyway." Of course, they both knew it wasn't windy that night.

A couple of months later (Halloween time!), Cory Combine was harvesting corn in a field not far from the old Austin place. Big John, the Fourwheel Drive Tractor, and Wally Wagon were also there to help.

As it started getting dark, they all decided to head for home. Just like Johnny and Billy, as they passed the old house, they heard strange noises. Buzzzz, rumBarumBa, Bang! Bang! Bang! And, just like Johnny and Billy, they ran scared all the way home!

When they entered the shed, they were still huffing and puffing. The others; Johnny, Billy, Peter Pickup, and Allie Gator were all there. "What's wrong with you guys? You look as if you have seen a ghost." said Peter. "I think we did," said Wally.

Now, Cory was the biggest and Big John was the strongest, but both of them and Wally were clearly scared. So Johnny asked, "Over by the old Austin house?" Surprised, Cory, Wally and Big John answered in one voice, "Yes. How did you know?"

"Well, the same thing happened to Johnny and myself a while back," said Billy. They were really starting to scare each other now. Peter added, "You know, I heard Farmer Fowler say that there has been a lot of activity around that old house lately."

"What's activity mean?" asked Allie. Allie was the youngest and she always tried hard to fit in. "It means someone or something is doing stuff over there," said Peter. Even though Allie was just as afraid as everyone else, she almost shouted, "You guys are silly. It's an empty old house. There's nothing to be afraid of!!!"

"Oh yeah!" said Johnny, "then why don't YOU go over there tomorrow and find out what's making those noises?"

"OK!" Allie said crossly. "But I'll go right now." And she left.

Johnny felt sad that he spoke harshly to her, but he knew there was something going on there.

Even from a distance, Allie could see a strange glow in the fog above the Austin place. Just as she was over the hill from the old house she started to hear the noises. "Clank, clank. Boom. Wizz." She was too afraid to go any further.

That moment, Johnny and the others showed up and Allie was quite relieved to see them!

"You're right, Allie," said Johnny. "We shouldn't be afraid of something just because we don't know what it is." So, with Allie leading the way, together they all went over the last hill and...

...were very surprised to see a large crew of workers with power tools, big work lights and paint, fixing up the old house. On the trip home they all laughed among themselves for letting their emotions get carried away. The very next day they were all really happy to hear that Farmer Fowler wanted Peter Pickup to go help a nice family move into the "old Austin" place!